THE VIRGIN'S BARGAIN

A BILLIONAIRE ROMANCE STORY

ELIZA DUKE

HOT AND STEAMY ROMANCE

CONTENTS

Blurb	v
1. Catherine	1
2. Sergei	8
3. Catherine	15
4. Sergei	22
5. Catherine	31
6. Sergei	37
7. Catherine	42
8. Sergei	50
9. Catherine	53
Sign Up to Receive Free Books	65
Preview of The Orphan Next Door	67
Emily	69
Grant	74
Other Books By This Author	89
Copyright	91

Made in "The United States" by:

Eliza Duke

© Copyright 2020 – Eliza Duke

ISBN: 978-1-64808-071-5

ALL RIGHTS RESERVED. No part of this publication may be reproduced or transmitted in any form whatsoever, electronic, or mechanical, including photocopying, recording, or by any informational storage or retrieval system without express written, dated and signed permission from the author

❀ Created with Vellum

BLURB

Catherine:

There are two men in my life right now; one of them I don't want to live without, and the other, I may die from. Morty Branch has been cyberstalking me for unknown reasons for six months and just announced that he knows where I live and is coming for me. I need help—fast. And the only man I have to turn to is the man of my dreams. But who is Sergei? How is he so confident that he can take care of my stalker problem? And how do I compensate him? I don't have anything to offer him that he wants besides my virginity—or so I think. When he comes up with a counter offer, it intrigues me. He'll protect me ...and in return, I'll be his for one week.

Sergei:

I just had a sweet, little virgin offer me her body in return for protection. Were I a lesser man, I would have taken her up on it. But I don't take advantage of desperate women—and this one is very desperate indeed. Instead, I lay down a simple rule: I will protect her in return for her living as my own for one lovely week. Her agreement is bound to make things interesting for me as I solve the mystery of her persistent, now murderous stalker. But when my own dark side of life frightens my Catherine away, I must find and save her before Morty Branch makes his move.

1

CATHERINE

I'm daydreaming about my neighbor, Sergei, when I check my email and the ten new messages shock me back to reality. All are from the same sender, all have attachments, and none of them do I want to open under any circumstances. The flesh-colored thumbnails at the bottom of my screen tell me enough.

The tall, dashing Slavic hunk who lives in the building penthouse vanishes from my mind for the first time in hours as I stand up from my desk chair. I can't deal with this right now. I leave the walk-in closet that serves as my computer nook and hurry into the kitchen to make myself a cup of tea.

I start crying a little as the tea brews in my tiny, purple, clay teapot. The tears have lots of fuel: confusion, grief, embarrassment, fear, shame, and even anger at both myself and the author of the emails. It takes a few minutes before I can force myself to stop.

Somebody help me, I scream inside my head. I've changed my email address five times in six months and changed my phone number four times. The authorities know; I send them everything he sends to me, but they have never done anything useful for me.

Morty, my stalker, started out as a friend I made online. I don't go out much at all, thanks to my health, and so I have almost no friends offline. I thought he was twenty and from my hometown back in Seattle. He told me that he was a fuel engineer at a plant my father used to own. He claimed that he got curious about me when I managed to make the papers a few times with my art.

Morty was polite and intelligent, completely unlike all those nauseating creeps I always end up blocking. He responded in ways that made it clear he was actually reading what I wrote and cared about my point of view. He made me feel safe, and so eventually, we got to exchanging —pictures—just normal ones, no nudes.

I'm shy about cameras. There's nothing particularly bad about my appearance, except of course for how young and vulnerable I look. I'm five-foot-nothing and slim, with wavy chestnut hair, pale skin, and big, light-brown eyes.

His photos show a guy a little older than me, who is a little weak-chinned and chubby, but kind-faced, with big, brown eyes and spiky, brown hair. He apparently liked nineties-era vintage clothes, including loose, light, stonewash jeans and trench coats. Not gorgeous, but I didn't care, especially at the time.

Not everyone can be the mysterious, wealthy man upstairs, whom I wish I could go back to daydreaming about again. I could have walked around in a happy haze this evening and gone to bed hugging my pillow and wondering what Sergei's thick, black hair smells like. Instead, here I am dealing with Morty's shit.

Again.

We spent almost a month corresponding online before he did anything ... off. But when he removed his cloak of civility, what a monster was revealed beneath. I don't know what exactly set him off after the end of that first month. I wasn't dating anyone else, so it wasn't jealousy. I didn't have an argument with him, do anything that he could possibly find insulting, or blow him off. But one day, out of the blue, he emailed me calling me a rich, crazy whore and told me that he wanted to fuck me with a knife.

I didn't believe it was Morty at first. It was such a complete change from the personality he had shown before that I was sure that someone had hacked his account! But no such luck. As soon as I wrote him on his Facebook to confirm, he repeated his horrifying threat, along with several more.

I was so shocked that I reported him at once, blocked his email address, and contacted the police. After furnishing copies of the threats to the cops, along with Morty's photos, I hoped that was the end of it. But, of course, it wasn't.

Morty has now been sending me threatening emails from different throwaway addresses for the last six months. Most of them are sexual, full of rape-porn images, and descriptive about what this raging creep wants to do to me as soon as he gets his hands on me. But, lately, it's getting to be a lot less porn and a lot more torture.

It's not just a matter of some guy being such a pissy fuckboy that I don't want to date him. This asshole is terrorizing me, and thanks to the things I foolishly confided—what can I say? I was lonely— he knows exactly how much his harassment is affecting me.

I've had PTSD with agoraphobia and panic attacks since my family died in an explosion when I was five. I don't like going outside, and I have trouble staying in rooms with more than four other people. Loud noises, especially fireworks, gunshots, or movie explosions can terrify me into a panic attack or worse—a flashback.

I take medication, meditate, exercise, see a therapist, and force myself to leave my home regularly. I'm still pretty much a shut-in, though. I'm not proud of this fact; I didn't even admit it to Morty until last month.

Fortunately, I received a big insurance settlement along with my inheritance from my parents. This lets me support myself, despite my problems. The apartment is big, secure, and luxurious, I have my own glassed-in balcony that I use as a greenhouse, and I even have a spare bedroom I was able to convert into a small art studio.

My life isn't too bad most of the time, although my friends are minimal, and the closest I have ever come to love is preoccupying myself with my mysterious neighbor. But in the age of the Internet, I can order almost everything I need online, from sushi to a ride to my therapist.

I take a deep, steadying breath and try to collect my thoughts. The chamomile tea is starting to fill the air with its sweet, delicate scent. I grab my favorite kitten mug and pour the golden liquid into it, then add a dollop of raw honey and stir.

I sip and read news on my phone silently for a while. Inside, I'm shoring myself up with the usual reassurances. Each one wears away a little bit at my fear, until I can think again.

Morty is a coward. All he ever does is talk. There's no chance that he will actually try to make good on any of these sick "promises" of his. None at all.

I am almost to the point where I could consider looking at those damn emails. But I stay there anyway, breathing deep and slow while I cast around inside my head for something else to focus on.

There's Sergei, at least.

Sergei, who lives in the penthouse, owns the building—among several others in the neighborhood. He is the kind of rich that even my father never aspired to, and no one has any idea how he came by it. There are so many rumors about our hot, aristocratic-looking landlord that I don't know where the truth lies.

Even so, thinking about him is like slipping into my jacuzzi: warm, relaxing, and leaving me tingling all over. It doesn't take all the fear and anger away, but it does rest my mind for a moment.

Is he a secret descendant of Russian aristocracy? Is he a criminal? Is he a reclusive artist? A novelist? A refugee from Putin's Russia made very, very good?

I have absolutely no way of knowing, and the mystery that shrouds Sergei makes him all the more attractive to me. Not that he needs any help in that department. He has all the intensity and athleticism of a military man and all the elegance of a man of breeding.

Tall and commanding, powerful in build, and meticulously well-dressed, he looks like the kind of man who lives in a castle, with a crown on his brow. Thick, wavy, jet-black hair spills around his strong, narrow face, with white skin, sensually curved lips, and narrow, deep-green eyes. His voice is deep and resonant, with a touch of a Russian accent.

I first ran into him when we shared an elevator on the way up from the lobby. I was coming from my afternoon therapy session, fragile-feeling and tired, and was relieved to have the mirror-walled elevator to myself. But before the doors closed, a tall figure in a black, wool overcoat stepped in through the gap.

I froze like a deer in my corner as he moved into the small space, his spicy cologne teasing my nostrils. He barely noticed me, busy with whatever conversation he was having on his cell phone. The conversation was in Russian, which I don't speak a word of, but the all-business tone to his voice was unmistakable.

I stared at the black curls that escaped from beneath his fur-trimmed hat as he rumbled authoritatively into his smart phone.

I glimpsed that narrow, intense face of his, but round, black sunglass lenses covered his eyes. I felt a strange, melting warmth, leaving my muscles loose but my heart pounding.

I wanted to ask who he was, but I didn't dare interrupt his phone call. I only found out later that this magnificent man was our landlord and the occupant of the building penthouse. By then, I already had a catastrophic crush on him.

I have never dared talk to him, not in an entire year of living here. I daydream about him when I take my walks, when I lie down for naps, or stretch out for the night's sleep. But aside from a curious glance now and again as I pass him in the lobby, Sergei Ostrov has never noticed me.

One day, maybe, I will get up the courage to talk to him in person. I have no idea what I'll say, but I want to try. Meanwhile, though, I'm forced to content myself with some very pleasant wishful thinking.

Daydreaming about Sergei does the trick; I'm smiling a little again by the time I finish my cup of tea. I get up to face the mess on my computer, bringing an extra mug of chamomile with me.

I let my eyes blur a little as I open each email in turn, avoiding the photographs. I don't know where this sicko, Morty, finds so many photographs of brutalized women, but I don't have to open them, and I never do. I send it all on to the cops and get it the hell out of my inbox.

Morty spends the first nine emails berating and threatening me in ways that are starting to become formulaic again.

Threats involving knives, kitchen implements, and sexual violation.

Demands that I answer.

Whiny pleas that I'm hurting his feelings by not answering.

All followed by more threats.

I hold my own through the nine-email tantrum and send them on without comment to my contact at NYPD. But then I open the last one, and the two lines of text send me into an instant panic.

The first line is my home address, along with the door code to my building. The second consists of four words:

I'm coming for you.

2
SERGEI

I'm standing in the corner of an underground meeting room, still and silent as a statue in one of my best dark, silk suits. My cousin, Mikhail, local boss for the Russian mob, sits casually at a desk at the front of the room. He smooths his white-blond hair back from his high forehead as he looks over the debtors that my men and I have brought to him. "Bring the first of them forward, Andrei."

Andrei, a brute with a blocky face and Russian prison tattoos, moves forward to lead the first of the serious debtors forward. It's Friday night: time to settle the weekly accounts. Each one owes us at least ten thousand dollars, and tonight they will either pay up or tell us how else they plan to compensate us.

There are seven of them, all races, all ages, all male, except for the underage-looking girl standing with one of the older men. My eyes rest on her for a moment; she's tiny, with innocent eyes and soft, undefined features. The man with her is skinny, twitchy, and very nervous. He's jonesing.

I wince, and Mikhail and I exchange glances before he turns to speak to the tiny, Arab man in the white, pillbox hat that Andrei brought forward.

A few of our "guests" have already noticed the plastic tarps lining the floor. An older man in a dull-brown suit keeps glancing down at them, tears clinging to the insides of his glasses. The girl stomps at a small wrinkle on one of the tarps and peers at it with a curious expression.

Someone has dressed her into a short, red, velvet dress that shows off her skinny shoulders and high-heeled shoes. The outfit's too old for her, as is the red lipstick she's wearing. This is a child, and from the way she is acting, she thinks this is all some kind of game.

One of my eyebrows twitches upward. The dozen of our men lounging against the walls start to notice my reaction and then what's causing it. They shuffle and mutter to each other in Russian, uncomfortable with the tiny girl's presence in a place where someone could easily get shot.

Even the hardest man in Russia has his limits. Kids are usually part of that. You don't mess with kids in our territory unless you are suicidal or completely stupid.

I'm not sure yet which one our debtor here is. But his forcing an oblivious little girl into this situation makes my blood boil. I'm no saint, but children and other such utter innocents are always off limits, no exceptions. One glance at Mikhail tells me that he's annoyed as well. Right now, though, we both have a job to do.

Mikhail calls each man forward in turn, working through the first three, extracting apologies, promises of payment, and in one case, a large bankroll. He tosses the latter to me and I riffle through it quickly: "Fifteen thousand even."

That guy, the weepy old man, goes free right away with a huge sigh of relief. The outer door of the warehouse we're in opens briefly, letting in a harsh beam of light, then creaks shut again after him.

The other adults seem relieved, understanding that my boss

is good as his word, and if they just pay up, that's the end of it. Of course, after today, things will get very complicated for those who try to drag their feet on paying. And the offers they make tonight will have to be pretty damn good.

When his time comes, the older man grabs the little girl by the upper arm and pulls her forward, a nervous smile on his lips. Mikhail stops leaning on the desk and unfolds his arms, peering at the man as he comes to a stop a few feet away.

"I don't have your money for you yet," the man stammers at Mikhail. "But I've brought you something to make up for it."

Before we can say anything, he puts his hands on the girl's shoulders and shoves her out in front of him. "Go," he orders her, and she looks back at him in confusion. "You are to go with these men, now!" he insists.

Mikhail and I look at each other again. I may not be entirely surprised, but that doesn't make me feel any less sick. Pushing out of my corner, I walk over to them.

The man's head snaps around, and his eyes widen as he sees me coming. I ignore him and crouch down in front of the little girl, looking into her soft, brown eyes. "Hello there," I say in English.

"Hi," she says, rocking a little and nibbling on one finger.

"How old are you?" I ask, keeping my tone as kind and calm as I can.

"She's fifteen—" the man tries to cut in. I snap my head around and fix him with a stare. Those who know me know that stare means danger. Those who don't know me typically think that stare means death. When it involves scum like this guy, that assumption is almost always right. Paling, he goes quiet. He glances around at the exits, as if assessing his chances of surviving a run for it.

"I'm eight," the girl pipes up, and the man looks at her in

horror. "Why did Uncle Willie say I was fifteen? Why do I have to go with you? Will my mommy be there?"

Barely marshalling my temper, I think of the girl's mother and the hell she's probably going through right now with her child missing. "I will take you back to your mommy as soon as this meeting is over," I promise. Again, I'm no saint, but I always keep my promises. It won't take me much effort to put her situation right.

Unfortunately, there's another part to the problem and he's losing all color in his face as I go quiet. The little one and her trash-fire of an uncle must be dealt with separately.

I turn my head to stare down the man, who is now looking between myself and the child with his mouth a perfect, mute 'O'. "You brought Mikhail an eight-year-old girl?"

"She's old enough," Willie stammered out after a moment. "I swear to God she's old enough. Just, please, take her! I don't got nothing else to pay my debt with!"

"So you kidnapped your niece, you dog?" I snap as I move back gently from the girl and stand up.

I can't stop glaring at this twisted, skinny little man with his meth teeth and his way of rubbing his face every few seconds. He's so grotesque, hunkered behind this child and begging that we take her ...for what? What kind of creatures does he think we are?

I know, though I hate it. He thinks that we are like him. No honor, no mercy, and no restraint of any kind.

"Please don't call Uncle Willie a dog," the girl says in her clear voice.

I look down, my eyebrow going up again, this time in amusement. "I'm sorry, what was that?"

"Please don't call Uncle Willie a dog," she pleads again. "That's mean to dogs. Dogs are nice."

I start to —laugh—but then hear Willie curse her under his breath. The bastard has only the smallest of ideas of how much trouble he's in. Immediately, I'm all business again. "Of course. Let me finish with your uncle, and I'll take you home."

I turn to Willie as I speak, and despite my kind tone in answering her, my eyes hold all my rage. His own eyes go round in absolute terror as the truth works its way through the meth, booze, and stupidity. He's fucked up worse than if he had just come here with turned-out pockets and a plea.

I gesture to one of our —men—Nicolai, a new father whose wife is a kindergarten teacher. "Nicolai, I've got a job for you," I call over in Russian.

Once Nicolai has gone to watch deliberately loud cartoons with Willie's niece a few rooms away, I turn to Willie, wearing my coldest expression. "You're living on your sister's couch, correct?"

Willie blinks in shock that I've done my homework. "Yeah," he mutters after a moment. "Why?"

"So, you conned your big-hearted sister into taking you in. Then, in return for her kindness, you menaced and then kidnapped her extremely underage daughter. Yes?" My accent gets thicker and my English worse the angrier I get, but Willie gets my meaning.

He gulped. "Wait, please, sir, just hear me out—"

"Hearing you out was exactly what Mikhail planned to do." I pull my Glock with its Glaser safety round loads from the holster beneath my leather blazer and hold it down at my side as he starts to shiver. "He still would, if you had not insulted his honor by implying that he would do anything to a child."

I point my pistol at his face and pull the trigger as he's drawing his breath to scream. The debtors who are still waiting to see Mikhail cringe as Willie's corpse falls to the floor, minus an eye. There is no exit wound. I feel no remorse. Yes, I am a killer. I kill street trash like Willie. And I will never regret it.

I look to Boris, another of my subordinates. "Get the cleaners up to take care of this before we bring the girl out," I order him as I go back to my corner. I know that rumors of this will get around, making sure that nobody ever tries to pay Mikhail in kidnapped children again.

It's almost midnight before I get the little girl, whose name is Amy, to walk up the street to the door of her Brooklyn brownstone and knock on it. She's none the worse for wear, with a tummy full of kid-sized cheeseburger and a strawberry shake. Her lack of interest in her uncle, given how sweet the little girl is, speaks volumes. She's not concerned about his wellbeing because, clearly, intuition told her he was a very bad man. Children know those things better than adults. They trust their instincts.

That's the last time that anyone ever saw—or will ever see-- Willie. The cleaners are very thorough. Anyone we kill disappears, thanks to them.

I watch through my spyglasses from behind my black Lexus as she pushes the intercom button and speaks for a while. Less than a minute passes before a short, round woman with Amy's hair bursts out the door and scoops her up into a hug, sobbing.

The woman lets out an explosive sneeze before turning and sweeping her child inside. In my head, I can put her bit of the story together, or at least make an educated guess. Mom, drugged out on cold medicine, trusted her brother to at least look after her kid. Whatever Amy tells her won't matter in the end; Willie's gone and the kid is safe. Hopefully her mother will never be so trusting again.

Willie died too fast and with too little pain. Maybe it's best that the poor woman slept through the most of it. If the police had already been there when I showed up, returning Amy would have been a lot tougher.

I'm done for the night. I get back in my Lexus and head toward my favorite bar in Central Park West, walking distance from my penthouse. I want a stiff drink and a woman for the night. I'll settle for the drink.

3

CATHERINE

I've tried to sleep for hours, ever since crying myself into exhaustion, but I can't. *Morty knows where I live.*

I don't know how he found me. He doesn't seem that good with computers, and I know I haven't left my information anywhere online. I'm too careful.

But he has my address, and now I must do something about it. Otherwise my home will never feel safe again. The only problem is, I have no one reliable to help me.

The police certainly don't count. They don't have a suspect to arrest, no one to file a restraining order against, and they won't spare an officer to watch over the building. I hung up after they suggested that at my income bracket I should have a bodyguard anyway.

They had a point, but having a bodyguard would mean letting some stranger into my life full-time. Thanks to my issues, the idea of sharing my precious apartment with some total stranger horrifies me.

But then I start to think about the apartment building where I live. Morty will have to get into it to get at me. If I can't get those who are supposed to protect the city to help me, maybe I can get the building owner to do something.

Sergei. I sit up in bed at the very thought, clutching the covers to my breasts. I'm considering finally talking to him, but doing even more than that: begging for his mercy and his aid.

He's wealthier than I have ever been. He doesn't need my money. But I should have something that he wants.

I still have my father's Matisse and Picasso and my mother's wedding jewelry, but I don't know how attractive an offer they will make for him. There's something else that I have that I'd rather give him, but using it in commerce makes me uncomfortable. I'm still a virgin.

These days, it's not unheard of. With the Internet providing anonymity and the ability to connect with people all over the globe, it's actually gotten fairly easy. A lot of young women sell their virginities.

But am I that mercenary? I know I'm that desperate, but do I have the nerve to do it? Would I even be considering it if I wasn't already so besotted? The answer to that last question, at least, is very definitely no. I'm no martyr.

I get up and get dressed in a bulky, snuggly, blue sweater and jeans,

It's probably very stupid for me to be wandering out in the middle of the night, now that my stalker is in town and knows my address. But I can't stay: the plan I'm considering is too crazy and I need to walk.

There's a bar two blocks from the apartment building. I'm not much of a drinker; the sedatives kill my tolerance and make it dangerous for me to drink too much. But there's one thing about that dark, little bar with all the gilding and mirrors that draws me far more than booze: Sergei goes there a lot.

When returning home from my evening therapy sessions, I have spied him bellied up to the bar or sitting at a corner table many times. I always look for him whenever I walk by its big, gilt-decorated window. When I see him, I always linger, drinking in the sight of him for as long as I dare.

I've always wanted to go in and have a drink. Maybe sit at that corner table and imagine what it would be like to sit there with him, drinking and talking ...like a couple on a date.

I bundle up, covering my hair and swathing myself in a dark, gray, wool overcoat that gives me a mannish look. I want no one to know who I am, or even that I'm female.

My heart starts beating fast as I make my way out the front door. It's been raining lightly, leaving the sidewalks more deserted than usual. New York is the city that never sleeps, but that doesn't mean the people here like getting soaked.

I walk the two blocks, looking around often, wary of anyone following me. No one does, or if they do, they're better at stalking than I am at picking them out. I force myself to trust that the latter isn't true as I spy the bar storefront up ahead.

There's a knot of drunken men on the sidewalk outside the door. I'll have to pass them to go inside. One of them swivels his head and locks his gaze on me like a targeting system as I approach, and my stomach starts flipping over.

He's ugly in a brutal way, his hair greasy and his face like a fist, except where his grin splits it. His tiny eyes are just gleams in the deep pits beneath his brows and he stumbles forward, grabbing for me as I get in range.

I step aside immediately and duck into the bar. I hear him curse behind me as the other men laugh at him. *Please, let that be the end of this.*

I glance around, but can't see any sign of Sergei. My heart sinks and I hurry toward a clear spot at the bar, knowing it will be harder for this creep to do anything if he's in full view of a lot of people.

I don't get three steps before a meaty hand closes on my upper arm. "I'm talking to you, bitch!"

Oh, God. My mind goes blank with terror; I stiffen up like a manikin as he starts dragging me backward. *No, don't touch me, leave me alone, someone help—!*

No one seems to notice as he drags me, mute and stiff with terror, toward the door. I want to cry out for help, but my voice sticks in my throat. I try to catch the bartender's eye, but he stares right past me as he polishes glasses.

My mind is starting to go blank, a flashback boiling up from the depths of my skull and filling my vision with flying rubble and fire. He's going to take me somewhere and rape me. No one is going to help—

"Stop right there."

The deep, accented voice is so familiar and unexpected that, for a moment, I wonder if I am dreaming.

The man stops and snorts, turning around while dragging me with him. When he sees Sergei standing in the doorway behind him, he goes very, very still.

I look up and the fire recedes from my brain as if blown out by a blast of icy air. Sergei stands there in his deep, blue, wool coat, hair loose on his shoulders, removing his fur-trimmed hat with one hand. The other hangs at his side casually, with a dark, snub-nosed revolver in it.

"Let the young lady go," Sergei rumbles, staying very calm, but staring unblinkingly into the older, fatter man's eyes.

The man looks over at me, his grip loosening a little already, and then turns his head again to take in Sergei. He licks his lips with a thick, purplish tongue, then lets me go.

"Should keep her closer if she's yours. Stupid little slut." He gives me a shove toward Sergei, and an iron hand shoots out to steady me as a whiff of spicy aftershave washes past my nostrils.

"She is not mine—the bar is. You are banned, *cacat*. Get out and do not return." He gives an imperious flick of the revolver, barely raising it from his side.

The man's jaw drops. He glances down at the revolver, then slinks out, giving Sergei a wide berth. I'm left standing frozen, right in front of the man of my dreams, with his hand still on my shoulder.

My heart is still beating fast, but the fact that he rescued me is sinking in.

He pockets the pistol as casually as a man putting away his cell phone, and concern breaks across his stern features. "Are you all right?" he asks.

My mouth opens, but my throat is still closed. I can't speak —yet, and to my deep surprise, his face falls as he instantly seems to recognize this. "No, clearly you are not."

He calls something in Russian over to the blank-faced bartender, who nods and lumbers into the back. Sergei ushers me over to the corner table and gets me sat down in a chair. A few moments later, the bartender comes over and sets a pot of steeping tea and a pair of cups on a trivet in front of me.

Sergei settles into the other chair to watch as I start to move and look around. "Are you back?" he asks in a low, calm voice after about a minute.

Something clicks into place inside of me, and I nod. "I ...am. Thank you." My voice is weak, but the words finally come out.

"You live in my building." It's not a question. He leans forward toward me, brow furrowing slightly. Then he nods once. "Catherine White, the heiress."

He doesn't mention the story behind my inheritance, though everyone who makes the connection between that name and my face knows the story. My parents' deaths, along with those of four-hundred-and-fifty-three other people, had made international news. I'm really glad that Sergei doesn't bring it up.

"Yes. I ...I have seen you around, but I'm bad at starting conversations." My cheeks tingle with heat, and I see him break into a faint smile.

"I am Sergei Ostrov, your landlord." He tilts his head, curiosity gleaming in his hard, green eyes. "What brings you out on the streets this late? It is not your normal habit."

I blink at him, words sticking in my throat again. He noticed my comings and goings? He actually knew that I existed all this time?

He chuckles at my amazement. "I make it a point to keep an eye on things around my properties. I do not abide outsiders disturbing the peace of my tenants."

The idea of him watching every night over his tiny kingdom makes me feel safer. "You ...watch over the neighborhood?"

"Not alone. I have a security team that assists in monitoring the ten blocks that I own." Ten blocks in Central Park West. That makes him a billionaire all by itself.

How did he make the money to break into the most lucrative real estate market on the Eastern Seaboard? *Yet another mystery.* He fascinates me more by the minute.

He pours the tea: some mixture of herbs, brewed very strong. I can smell chamomile in there somewhere. He slides a cup over to me, and I take it, warming my fear-chilled hands on it. My eyes dart to his own hands, so large and, from a few minutes back when one rested on my shoulder, so warm.

He pours for himself. "Something upset you, I suspect, or you would not have left the haven of your home. Am I correct?"

I pause with my trembling cup halfway to my lips, then set it down. He watches me and waits, neither coaxing me nor changing the subject. Finally, I manage to nod.

I'm drained from fighting flashbacks= and still not quite sure how I should approach him. But there's no choice ...and if he has an interest in tenant security, he should know about the threat to it.

"I need your help, Mr. Ostrov."

4

SERGEI

"Come in," I tell Catherine, leading her in through the entrance of my penthouse. I hear her draw a sharp breath as she takes in all the carved wood and floor-to-ceiling bookshelves. Then she walks past me through the door, clutching her leather book bag to her chest. She is incredibly vulnerable, and yet, not in a way that makes her weak. Though afraid, she's come directly to me for something. Men frequently refuse to do any such thing. I immediately appreciate her courage.

"Thank you for hearing me out," she murmurs, not quite cringing, but both shy and a touch deferential. I am left wondering what has left her so timid.

"You said it is a security matter. If it happens on my property, it concerns me." I lead her through the enormous living room and into my office, which takes up one corner of the floor.

Three walls of the office are covered with state-of-the-art

computer equipment, including an entire wall of monitors. Each one shows a different camera feed: the lobby and hallways of the apartment building, its side alleys, two views of its entryway, and one of its rear exit. The street beyond feeds from other buildings, and there is even a feed from the bar. I can see it all from behind my desk.

I SIT down there and gesture to a leather office chair across from mine. She settles herself into it and looks up at me, and I know there's a lot more going on with this girl than random encounters with piggish drunks.

"I HAVE A STALKER," she starts. "He's been threatening me for six months. This morning he—he sent me my address and our building's door code and wrote that he's coming for me."

"HMMM." I don't know what I was expecting, but this wasn't it. How does a girl as reclusive as this one get a stalker? The notion troubles me unaccountably. "I'll have that code changed right away. Would you be willing to show me these correspondences?"

SHE ACTUALLY HAS a file folder of printouts tucked away in her bag, as if she's making her case to a lawyer or mayor. The touch of formality and her respectfulness disarm me just as much as her pretty face and shy sweetness. I sit at the desk and page through the emails and message texts, and of course, the incredibly tacky porn and gore photos. In my line of work, I'm wholly desensitized to most things. However, the thought of any of the images in these photographs being replaced by Catherine's sweet face ... my gut tightens and I tamp down a flare of rage.

"Why do stalkers always talk so damned much?" I grumble, and she lets out a little, nervous laugh. "But I'm more confused by his targeting you at all. As far as I can see, you had no conflict with him."

"No. I ...I thought he liked me." I can hear her confusion. "Did I do something else wrong?"

I scoff. "You are one of the most inoffensive women I have ever met." And that's saying something. I'm quite easily offended. Dangerously so. "I doubt you have even argued with anyone online."

"No, I try to use reason, and if someone gets abusive, I just block them. But he keeps persisting, almost as if he has some personal vendetta." She looks at me pleadingly, those big, soft, golden-brown eyes of hers affecting me like a caress.

I can tell when a lady desires me, and this little one has been giving me longing looks whenever we cross paths for the better part of a year. I have never flirted with her, but that is only because she seems delicate, and getting drawn too deeply into my life might break her. I have broken many men. Women, I am more careful with. And this woman in particular—I don't want to see her suffer in any way, much less at my hands.

. . .

I LOOK BACK DOWN at the printouts and then put them back in their folder. "This man would be very foolish to come onto my property seeking to do violence. I will not permit it." I watch her face as I make this declaration and see her melt a little, something like adoration sparkling in her eyes.

NOW HER GAZE feels like a caress again—all up and down my cock. In that moment, all my good intentions vanish. As I said, I am not saint. I decide, right then and there, to seduce her. I can't promise her anything but a good time and my full protection, but I know I can make certain she enjoys it.

LATER. *Business first.* "I can do a great deal against him, depending on what you want to happen. Name the level of response that you wish, and I shall make it happen—for a price, of course."

"I'M NOT sure what it will take to stop him, but I don't care what it is as long as it means I don't have to fear him anymore." She licks those pale, rosebud lips, and I feel a catch in my chest. "As for the price ...I'll do whatever is necessary. I just want him gone."

I CAN SYMPATHIZE. "You understand that this may mean that force must be used." I'm forced to walk around the issue. I do not know yet if the girl can keep a confidence, though I suspect she can and will.

. . .

"I know that stalkers usually can't be reasoned out of what they are doing." She shifts nervously, forcing herself to turn her wandering gaze back to me. "You must know more how to handle these things than I do."

I nod and lean back in my seat, shuffling through the papers a last time before laying them aside. "Whoever this person is, they are obsessed, but the obsession is not sexual."

That surprises her—and I see a look of understandable relief. There are worse things that a man can do to his victim besides kill her. "Oh. But ...what, then?"

"The foulness of the messages is simply another psychological attack. This man does not desire you. He desires to make you afraid."

She lets out a shivering breath, and I make a mental note to make her stalker suffer for instilling that fear in her "It's working."

"Then you require more intensive protection." I'm not sure what exactly it is I am proposing, but I know that I haven't had a good woman look at me like she does in too long. I thirst for her adoration even more than I do for her slim body. "But I must ask how you plan to compensate me for my trouble."

"What do you want?" she asks very softly as she gazes up at me. "I have a Matisee—"

"I do not need money, nor valuables." The idea continues to form: something audacious, but appealing—hopefully to both of us. But I hold off on proposing it, waiting to see what else she offers.

"I ...have only one other thing that might interest you," she admits. More hesitation. More shy looks. "I have something that many men consider to be of great value."

She is blushing again and I wait, one eyebrow lifting slightly. "What is it?" I keep my tone gentle.

It seems to take all her courage to look back into my eyes. "I am a virgin, sir."

While the admission doesn't surprise me at all, the kick of ravenous lust does. I have watched the buying and selling of virginities online, on various Deep Web sites. The need for young women to sell themselves to survive—it disgusts me as much as any vile crime I've seen in my years on the job. And yet, here is small, sweet, lovely Catherine, offering her virginity up to me as collateral for my protection. For one brief second, that notion appeals and I'm reminded that, in spite of my attempt to steer clear of many common street vices, I am still the same as every other criminal. Thankfully, my iron self-control kicks in just as quickly as initial desire.

I CATCH her gaze and hold it. "Catherine, as lovely an offer as that is, I can't accept sex as payment from you."

SHE LOOKS —shocked—and then mortified. Her eyes go bright and she can't look at me anymore. "Have I disgusted you?"

"No, no." I keep my voice warm. I'm still deciding what I want from her. She will not leave me with my desire unslaked. But some things will never be currency with me. "It is simply that I do not take a woman into my bed who does not fully want to be there."

SHE OPENS HER MOUTH, and for a moment I wonder if she will finally admit to her crush. "I ..." she manages, but then pales and can't go on. "I understand, but I have nothing else."

"Do NOT CONCERN YOURSELF. I am delighted that you would entrust me with such a gift." I wait a beat, then make my counter-offer. "I propose a trade. Work for me for one week, starting tomorrow, and I will make your stalker problem go away forever."

. . .

SHE STARES at me in amazement. "What work ...will I be doing?" Her voice has a note of hope in it again ...and of wild curiosity.

THE IDEA COMES to me without preliminaries, as do all my best plans. "You will serve me," I purr, holding her gaze.

HER EYES WIDEN. "HOW?"

"YOU WILL LIVE with me and be at my disposal every hour of every day, aside from your periods of needed rest. In short, outside of certain limits which you may set, you will do whatever I ask. Wear what I wish, act as I wish, and read and learn what I wish."

"BUT NOTHING SEXUAL." Is that a note of disappointment? Yes, I am almost certain of it.

I SMILE and brush my fingertips over the back of her hand before drawing back again. "I won't touch you in that way until you want it enough to ask me for it, straight out." I wink at her. "No exceptions."

THAT MAKES her relax a little more; evidence of principles always helps put a lady at ease. The adoring look is back in her eyes, and for once, I feel as though I've done a small good thing, albeit coupled with plenty in it for me.

She considers my offer. "One week."

· · ·

"Yes. With the conditions negotiated ahead of time." The smile I offer is lazy and sensual this time. "Say tomorrow, over breakfast?"

It takes her a few moments longer to decide. When she does, she peeks at me again from beneath her lashes before steeling herself and looking me in the eyes. "I'll do it."

5
CATHERINE

Sergei sets two large men in bland, dark suits to guard my door from the outside as I sleep. He warns me to avoid preoccupying myself with Morty's messages, and I try to take it to heart. I do glance at my phone and see three unknown-sender messages and ten more emails from a fresh throwaway account.

I can handle leaving them unread. The terrible mix of fear and fascination that left me glued to Morty's messages has vanished. Sergei will protect me now ...and his offer commands all of my attention.

I know what dominance and submission are. I have read enough about them online. Some people structure their whole relationship around the dynamic, while others reserve it for the bedroom. Sergei seems to be the former.

The whole idea leaves me lying awake for a while, mind racing and toes curling. What will it be like to let him take control? He promised to allow me whatever limits I need to feel comfortable.

Take the fear of abuse out of the equation, and it's ...actually tempting. Somehow, I know that Sergei will never hurt me. That was corroborated by his refusal to accept my virginity as repayment for protecting me, something that both frustrated and relieved me. Mostly, though, I'm grateful. He wants enthusiasm from me, not desperation.

He attracts me even more just by showing that he wants me too and cares about what I want when he doesn't have to. I expected power and command from him. I didn't expect thoughtfulness, protectiveness, or honor.

I swear this crush I'm getting on him is going to kill me.

My phone chimes softly: a message. I check it eagerly, wondering if it is Sergei. No such luck; it's that unknown number again. I leave Morty to rant into my answering service again, feeling more annoyed and disgusted than afraid.

Sergei is right. Morty doesn't want me; he wants to terrorize me. But now he's the one who will get to feel terror. I have no doubt that Sergei can be terrifying if he chooses to be.

I would love to see Morty cry in terror. It's not very kind of me. But after all the nights of fearing him and suffering my usual symptoms ten times worse because of the stress, I want Morty to feel fear and pain as well.

I guess I've reached my limit with all this craziness. It's starting to affect my morals. I just want this over with before it changes me too much.

The chimes go off about every ten minutes for the rest of the night. I don't even look at my phone after the third one. I give Sergei's messages and calls their own tones, turn down the chime for Morty, and put the phone in my open nightstand drawer to muffle the sound a little.

I think of Morty calling and texting all night long, getting himself into a helpless froth. I think of him coming here and trying to storm the place, only to be shot by the two armed men guarding my door like a bank vault. Now that Sergei is taking the fear away, I smile at the thought and sleep soundly It's the first time in months I've slept in more than three-hour stretches, interrupted by panic, followed by a few more hours of restless sleep.

Morty left eight more phone messages before my message box filled. Two hundred more texts are waiting for me. On Sergei's orders, I don't look at them and I find that I feel better for obeying.

I grew up Upstate, in my aunt's museum-like old home, so I'm used to being up at dawn. I get up and shower, my head full of cotton from last night's late hours. I don't mind. I finally feel ...safe.

If I make myself Sergei's, as I dreamed of doing, I will be safe from everyone else. It shocks me to feel so comfortable with handing myself over to a near stranger. It's the crush; it's addling my thoughts.

The bliss recedes a little bit as I shower off and start to wake up. I remember the warm feelings, only a fraction as strong, that I felt when I thought that Morty cared about me. They were enough to deceive me into trusting him too much.

They were also weak and insignificant compared to what I feel for the man I'm offering the reins of my life to. This is New York City. Predators are everywhere, and I still know nothing substantial about Sergei.

What if I can't trust him? What if I'm wrong again? Do I really know what I'm signing up for? Sergei would be a far more terrifying stalker than Morty could ever be.

I could be right in putting my trust in him. It could be amazing—an adventure.

But it could also be the doorway to a hell worse than the one I'm currently in.

I stand there frozen under the hot spray, trembling with sudden terror. My heart can't take another hit. After the explosion, a decade and a half of loneliness and sickness, and then

Morty as the cherry on top of the whole shit sundae, I'll break. I'll snap in half like a weathered board and crumble like sawdust.

I close my eyes and hunt for solid ground inside of myself. *Catherine, it's only a week. You fantasized about trying with this guy for almost a year.*

Do I want to try it, go through with this week and see where it leads, and very likely ensure my safety in the process? Or do I want to back out and hide in my home until Morty comes to put me out of my damned misery?

I have one scrap of pride too much to cave in like that. I steady myself against the wall of the shower stall, open my eyes, and lift my head. Sergei's beautiful, hard, handsome face moves into my vision, followed by a rush of heat as I imagine how strong the rest of his body must be.

I'm seeing this through. I'll face the consequences of my choice, no matter what they are, like everybody else does. If it turns out that I've fucked up, at least I'll take pride in the fact that I made a decision, instead of letting my fear and sickness make all my choices for me.

As I'm drying off, I hear a knock at the door. "Miss White, your clothes for the day have been delivered. Please come to receive them."

I blink in confusion as I wrap myself in my fluffy, white robe and head for the door. I open it, and one of the men turns to me with a small, polite smile. "Mr. Ostrov says you are to put this on and then join him upstairs for breakfast. You are to also bring your laptop and cellular telephone."

I hesitate, then accept the large, white cardboard box he offers. "I'll be out as soon as I can."

I don't open the box until I swallow my meds, take my vitamins, drink a big glass of water, and brush and pin up my hair.

Then, I walk up to my bed where I have set it and gingerly lift the lid.

Inside is a sheath dress in heavy, woven burgundy silk. It has long gloves in place of sleeves and an artfully draped Grecian bodice, which emphasizes the mounds of my breasts without baring them. Matching boots with low, riding-style heels, simple silk hose, a garter belt, bra, and panties in soft rose complete the ensemble.

There's a jewelry box tucked in with the outfit, and I check it after a moment. White gold earrings set with emeralds gleam back at me. *Holy shit*, I think, and hastily start to get ready.

I don't have time to admire myself in the mirror very long, but I do stop and stare for a few moments. This is Sergei's idea of a breakfast outfit? I am terrified that I will spill on it, but ...

...I also have never seen myself look so beautiful before.

I look a moment longer, touching my now braided-up hair and the dangly earrings. Good enough. I don't want to keep him waiting.

Sergei is waiting for me in the hallway, dressed in a black silk suit and a burgundy tie that matches my dress. He looks so good that the heat from the shower seems to suffuse me all over again. He looks me over and nods his approval. "Good. You know how to follow instructions. I presume that you have not answered your phone?"

"No."

He holds out a hand for the phone and laptop, and after a moment's hesitation, I hand them over. There goes my social life until he is done with whatever modifications he has planned, but ...there also goes Morty's only way of accessing me.

"Good." He already has my lock screen pass code, and he opens my phone, flicking through a few screens. He scowls. "He continues to try and reach you, I see. Good. The angrier and more desperate he is, the more likely he is to make a mistake."

He offers his arm and I take it; he tucks my laptop under his other arm, pocketing my phone. "I have a surprise for you, my dear."

"The last few hours have been full of surprises," I murmur, and he chuckles as he leads me to the elevator.

It's unseasonably warm this morning, as I discover when we step out of the elevator. Walking out under the sky shocks me for a moment; I didn't realize that the elevator had roof access. But then again, this space, like Sergei's penthouse, is obviously private.

A broad, brightly-tiled plaza spreads before us, containing a covered barbecue and cooking area, a gazebo with a dining table, and a jacuzzi. Beyond and around it, a rooftop garden sprawls, trimmed back in spots to start preparing it for autumn. Flowers still bloom in every corner of the garden, spilling from pots and troughs full of rich, damp earth.

The smell intoxicates me. Here, so far above the stink of traffic, the loam and chlorophyll and floral scents all mix in my nostrils, and I smile as he walks me to the gazebo. "It is beautiful up here."

"I always take my meals here when weather allows," he rumbles as he settles into a seat and lays the laptop and phone on the tabletop. "But business first."

One of his men steps forward with a small, black briefcase, from which Sergei pulls out a sheaf of papers and the folder with my evidence on Morty. "First, we formalize our agreement. Then, we go through the information available and make our plans."

I swallow and press my thighs together under the table as I sit across from him. He slides the sheaf of papers over to me, and I see that it is a contract.

6

SERGEI

It takes ten minutes for Catherine to sign herself over to me for a whole week. I can barely conceal my pleasure at her giving herself into my hands. But my seduction of her must be artful and happen on her timing, not my own.

There are limits, of course. She knows enough to ask for a safe word to veto any act she cannot complete without significant discomfort. I choose to believe that I would have asked her to select such a word if she hadn't asked for one. Surely there is that much decency left in me.

Her other limits are, for the most part, things that shouldn't even have to be said. No giving her to another. No forcing her to serve anywhere but in private. No preventing access to her medical needs, her friends, or the haven of her home.

It says a lot about how much this man has violated her that she thinks she has to defend the most basic of her rights. I have already decided to kill him, but I haven't decided whether to tell her about it. I do not want to upset her —further—and she has made it clear that she cares more about the end than the means.

Of course, that doesn't mean she can handle contemplating

what those means are. But that is not her duty. It is mine. For now ... she is my duty. I find I like that idea very, very much.

I sit back in my chair, looking down at the ink of her signature as it dries on the paper, its wet gleam fading. Catherine is nibbling on a bowl of fruit, yogurt, and granola across the table from me. I sip my coffee, unwilling to call for my plate yet.

Mikhail already knows about the stalker problem, and men are on the streets and watching local hotels for Morty. If he is in town, he will be caught before the week is up. Meanwhile, I am having Xenia, one of my assistants, research him online after she checks Catherine's laptop.

With all that delegated, I turn my attention to the phone. Catherine pauses and sets her spoon down nervously, looking up at me.

"I'm going to listen to those messages now."

She nods, and I put the phone to my ear, listening dispassionately to a few minutes of threats and pleading. Morty has a high, whiny voice with a slight quaver to it—almost womanish. Something about it bothers me, but I haven't put my finger on what yet.

I make a few mental notes. "Do you have other ways of contacting your friends besides this phone?"

"Facebook. I have no relatives I'm in touch with. Just a few friends." It's more information than she needs to volunteer.

"You'll have your computer back within the hour. This telephone, however, I will need for at least the rest of the evening. We will be seeking to trace his calls."

"Of course."

"Good." And just like that, the phone starts ringing with the softest chime. I check and notice that she has designated a very quiet tone for Morty. "And here he is. Let's get this part over with."

She gapes as I connect the call. I see her about to —protest

—and then, at my glance, she fights down the urge. I give her a small smile of approval. "Trust me," I mouth, waiting for the voice on the other end of the line.

"Catherine? Where are you, bitch?" comes the high, nasal voice. It sounds a little slurry. I suspect he's drunk. Drunkenness is no excuse for being slovenly and uncivil, however. This animal is both things. "You just gonna sit on the phone and not say anything?"

I put every bit of my disgust with this creature into my expression for Catherine's benefit, but my voice stays businesslike. "If you are looking for Catherine White, you can stop."

The startled squawk clashes again somehow with the look of the barrel-chested man in the photos. *I'm missing something here.* Silence for a few moments, and then the voice growls, "Who is this?"

"Sergei Ostrov," I reply smoothly. To those who do not move in my circles, it means nothing; to those who do, it means everything.

"Who the fuck is that?" he rasps. Definitely not a local career criminal, or connected to any. His ignorance will be his demise. "Where's Catherine?"

"She is no longer your concern." My voice is cold and firm. "You will not have the opportunity to trouble her again. If you should try, you will face consequences."

I hear whoever it is start to breathe fast and heavy before I even finish my statement. "You—!" he starts.

I cut him off with a tone like steel ringing off of ice. "This is not negotiable. You are alone, and I am not. You are unconnected and powerless, and I am quite the opposite. I have Catherine. She is my possession. *I will kill anyone who tries to take her.*"

Catherine gasps; I glance at her and see her staring at me in adoration mixed with complete shock. I hang up without waiting on Morty's response.

"For the record," I purr at her as I reach across the table and briefly toy with a wisp of her hair. "No, I don't think that my little speech will scare him off. But the gauntlet has now been thrown. Soon enough, I will take his hatred of you and turn it against me instead."

She stares at me as if I'm not speaking English any more. "Is that safe?"

I can't help it; I laugh. "No. But neither is life. And besides, little one ...he has much more reason to fear me than I have to fear him."

The servants bring me my steak, eggs, and toast, and she and I dine together. She doesn't talk much yet, but the amazed looks she keeps shooting me speak volumes. I find myself wanting to see more of the same every day.

She has a doctor's appointment that afternoon; I send two of my men to drive her and go to meet Mikhail and Xenia about her while she is gone.

Mikhail is lounging in a white turtleneck and jeans in the game room of his mansion. Half-Mongolian Xenia sits at a desk in the corner, tapping away at Catherine's laptop. They both look up as I walk in. Mikhail smiles broadly, and Xenia readjusts her large, round glasses and goes immediately back to work.

"Ah, cousin, how is your new pet project going?" He's the only one who I have told everything to.

"Well, thus far. Her stalker is no professional, and I doubt he has any local connections. I suspect he is yet another puffed-up basement-dweller who will show up with one of his mother's kitchen knives and have no idea what to do with it." We both laugh.

"Well, I do wish you luck." He coughs into his fist. "After the show you put on last night, all the debtors settled their debts at once. I only wish they were this cooperative every week."

I remember the little girl and her uncle's corpse, forcing a smile. I've quietly ensured that both she and her mother will be permanently protected and provided for until she turns 18. "I am happy to be of help to you, cousin."

"Sergei," Xenia calls with a surprising amount of urgency in her voice. Mikhail and I both look up, then head in her direction. As we approach, she turns on the screen projector and sends a larger version of the desktop onto the pull-down projection screen.

"I have set up her laptop with appropriate security and found out everything I could about her stalker. Morty Branch. I found him using his social media information, but ...there's a problem." Her bird-like black eyes meet mine.

"What is it?" I ask as Mikhail watches, fascinated.

"Morty Branch, age forty-five, formerly employed by White-Corp as an engineering intern." She gestured to the screen full of links and listed information. "Son of a single mother who still lives in Seattle."

"So he worked for her parents. I presume he is older than twenty, then." Of course. He didn't have a taste for nineties — style—those photographs were from the nineties.

"Well ...about that. This person currently has social media accounts, a PayPal, and even a few credit cards in his name. But according to Washington State Vital Records, he can't possibly be Miss White's stalker."

My brow knits. "No?"

"No, sir." She sits back and readjusts her glasses. "Morty Branch has been dead for the better part of two decades. He died in the same explosion that killed Catherine's parents."

7
CATHERINE

"He's ...dead?" I stare at Sergei in amazement, not sure what to think. The report from Sergei's research expert sits on the coffee table in front of me; its wording is very plain. "But ...if the real Morty is dead, then who ...?"

"I have my suspicions." He pushes off his living room wall and walks over to me, settling onto the black, leather couch next to me. "I do not believe that he was chosen at random. Not with his ties to your parents."

The closer he gets to me, the warmer and more electric the space between us seems to get, like sparks are dancing between our bodies. I swallow and recross my legs, glad for the mild distraction from my cold frustration. "We really don't know anything about him, outside to his having some tie to the real Morty."

"Have faith. I have protected many and destroyed more." He reaches out and touches my hair again. It's the tiniest bit of contact, but enough to make me tremble. I want to lean into his hand and feel it pressed fully against my skin. But I'm not brave enough. Not yet. "This person will not remain hidden from me long."

"I believe you."

It has been a day since we made our agreement, and I am already in agony. Not because I do what he says and not because I am in his house. No; it is because I can't yet force myself to ask him, straight out, to fuck me.

I can excuse offering Sergei my body if I need to do it or if he orders me to do it. But that is not what he wants from me. He wants me to want it wholeheartedly. He wants me to tell him, in clear terms, to fuck me.

I wish I could push myself to say it right away. I want it—I'm just so shy and I don't know how to ask. But his requirement echoes in my ears again, and I know I must work up the nerve to comply to get what I want.

It's the only order he's given me so far that I have chafed at, and the craving for him only grows because of it. It's enough to distract me some from the crazy news and keep it from overwhelming me.

"So, nothing I know about my stalker is true." It's still a shock.

Sergei lets out a grunt and nods. "I wish that I had better news for you. But I believe that your stalker's choice of using Branch as his cover identity is significant in itself. He was a former employee of your parents and died in the same plant explosion that killed them." He keeps his tone gentle. "It stands to reason that your gentleman caller is someone close enough to Morty to want to avenge his death."

"But ...why attack me to get back at my parents? I wasn't even involved, and they're dead!" My voice is rising, and I catch it. I press my lips together and close my eyes.

His hand brushes my back gently—dare I even say, tenderly? I open my eyes and see him looking at me with a kind of compassion that I'm sure few people have seen on his face. I feel ... privileged. "It is outrageous that you became a target for vengeance. You're one of the few people I have ever met who truly means no harm to anyone." There's something wistful in his tone, and it calms me a little bit, despite the subject.

I don't like thinking about That Day, let alone discussing it. Too much of that and the memories might crowd forward and overwhelm my sense of the here and now. I don't have flashbacks very often nowadays, but when I do, they are still monsters.

"Are you well, little one?" Sergei asks in such a concerned tone that it startles me.

I blink mutely, then swallow and shake my head. At once he reaches over and cups the side of my face. His huge, long-fingered hand with its palm like soft leather slides over my jawline, then moves up to unpin and loosen my hair.

I catch my breath. It's been a long time since anyone touched me that wasn't a doctor. I can't even remember the last time someone was tender with me. My skin prickles under his touch as he unravels my braid, as if sleeping nerve endings are waking up.

"It will be all right," he reassures me. "Trust me, little one. I will make the connection, and I will stop this man. I will protect you. You have my word."

I lean my cheek into his palm and look up at him pleadingly, my mouth dry and my body tingling all over. I ache for more of his touch. *Make love to me*, I try to say, but it's stuck in my throat.

He sees the look in my eyes and the corners of his eyes crinkle with amusement. "Tonight, you and I must forget this whole matter for a while and enjoy ourselves." He doesn't qualify how, and my own handy suggestion still won't come out of my mouth.

I keep trying to get words out and finally have to change the subject. "I was wondering ..." I start, having problems with my eye contact again. "I know almost nothing about you. Do you mind if I ask you some personal questions?"

"Only if you answer my questions as well." He toys with my hair again, and I shiver and lean into his touch.

"Of course." I peek at him through my eyelashes. "If you ask me anything, I must answer you either way, right?"

He gives me that amused smile that warms me so much and nods. "I suppose. But ...I'll be indulgent." He wraps a few strands of my hair around his fingers, and I get the sudden mental image of him grabbing a fistful of it and holding it firmly.

I let my head fall back, not yet finding my voice, then let out a soft whimper as he grips my hair obligingly. *Yes, like that.* I bite my lip, squeezing my legs together, and for a moment, I almost think that I can find the nerve to tell him.

"Can you speak?" he purrs as he holds me near the scalp, firmly and without pain. The tension gathering in my belly makes it hard to respond for a moment.

All this from just a little hair pulling. What have I been missing? I gasp for air, then say, "Yes..."

"What did you want to know?" His voice is mellow, as if he has no clue what his grip, closeness, and musky, spicy scent are doing to me.

"Why did you decide to help me?" I don't want it to sound suspicious, but there's still that fear in the back of my head.

He pauses, then lets out that same little chuckle. "You intrigue me. I want to see what happens if I coax you out of your shell."

That surprises me. I imagined he would claim boredom, or a desire to have a pet for a week, or simple territoriality against a problem trying to bring itself to his door. "I'm ...not that special."

He lets my hair go and withdraws, scowling. I blink up at him, shocked and aching from the lack of contact, then freeze when I see anger in his eyes. But instead of shouting, or doing anything violent, he speaks in a quiet but powerful voice.

"If you show disrespect to someone who I have chosen to invest my time and effort in, you show disrespect to me. You will break yourself of this habit of speaking ill of yourself. Humility is a virtue, but don't you dare run yourself down."

He stares into my eyes a moment longer, as a bittersweet mix of awe, shock, and gratitude washes over me. Once the shock wears off enough, I swallow and nod.

"Good," he replies. "Now. My turn. I know that you have no enemies; no one could hate you unless they were insane. But what about your parents? Did they have any enemies?"

"I don't really know," I admit after a moment's thought. "I was so small back then. None of the news reports or legal proceedings that I looked up afterward mentioned any problems with anyone. Some of the families of the people lost in the factory explosion wanted to sue, but the estate settled all that."

I realize that I am clenching my fists when my nails dig into my palms. I look down and try to relax them, but they won't, until Sergei reaches forward and covers my hands with his. I take a deep breath ...and feel my nails pull free and my knuckles stop aching.

"Are you with me?" he asks very gently, and after a moment, I nod.

"It just gets hard to talk about sometimes," I admit. "I don't usually have flashbacks any more, but sometimes they creep up on me when the accident comes up. It's not as bad as it used to be, though."

He nods and holds my hands until I can breathe again. I want to kiss him for it, but instead, I keep my mind on getting back to normal.

"How do you know how to deal with someone having attacks like this?" I ask finally.

His smile fades and he glances away. "My mother was a Romanian who fled to join relatives in Russia after her parents were taken by the secret police. She was there; she hid under the bed for over a day before one of the neighbors found her. From that day, she would be struck down by serious attacks at least a few times a week."

It shocks me. I can't imagine him coming from someone who was that broken. He seems made of iron.

"By the time that I was born, she no longer had such severe episodes. But now and again, she still would, and my father made certain I knew how to help her focus back on reality." He gives my hands a squeeze, then leans back, withdrawing his touch and leaving me aching again.

"I'm grateful."

He nods once, then the corner of his mouth curls up. "How long have you had a crush on me?"

I freeze inside, choking on my words, only managing to let out a small, embarrassed squeak. His eyes twinkle with amusement at the sound, and he just ...waits.

Damn it. "I ..." Heart pounding, palms damp, shaking inside, I screw together all my courage and barely manage to rise to the occasion. "Since the night I first saw you. In the elevator."

"The elevator?" He sounds intrigued ...and confused.

"You were on the phone and stepped in just as the doors were closing." Of course he had not noticed me.

"Ah, I see." He tilted his head slightly. "How long ago was that?"

"Almost a year." I'm blushing again. *Damn it.* I need to distract him from me and my ridiculousness. "So ...what do you do for a living?"

"Besides real estate?" His smile has faded, surprising me.

"Yes," I say, wondering why my stomach is tightening.

He hesitates, eyes searching my face. "I lead ...a large private security team." He's choosing his words carefully. I find myself wondering if it's a euphemism for something. "I have done it for almost two decades."

A private security team? For who? An eccentric billionaire? A criminal mastermind? I want so much to pry further, but the look in his eyes stops me. He looks ...a little worried, as if he's wondering if my interest in him will survive learning his secrets. Abruptly, I realize that this man of steel also has vulnerabilities. Oddly, it leaves me feeling even safer with him.

I get my laptop back the evening of the next day, scanned for viruses and other issues, and with every scrap of correspondence with "Morty" copied from it. Once I am done with the evening's duties and another long, agonizingly flirtatious after-dinner conversation with Sergei, I take it back to the sumptuous guest room Sergei has given me.

It has been an interesting day. I must accept all Sergei's orders, but mostly what he has had me do is tell him about myself, wear what he pleases, and keep him company. I spent the whole time struggling to tell him that, *yes, I want you. Please take me to bed now.*

He is kind, but firm. He never frightens me and only rebukes me when I speak badly of myself.

I'm honestly not sure if I want it to end once the week is up.

I check in on Facebook and let people know that I'm all right, but will be scarce for about a week thanks to the flu. Then I check my emails.

I have one in my inbox that is from an unknown sender. I freeze. I'm no longer afraid of this person's threats, but I know I need to tell Sergei about it. I promised.

But curiosity finally gets the better of me and I open it.

Do you know who you're whoring out to? Google Sergei Ostrov.

My throat tightens. I shouldn't be giving weight to anything that this fake Morty tells me. But the problem is that I already have doubts. I'm already dead curious—so much so that I'm wondering why I didn't do a search on him before.

I've offered him my life for a week. I'm thinking of offering him my body and maybe even my heart. But I can't afford to do that while knowing nothing real about him except that he's rich, protective as hell, and loves his mom.

I run the search.

Instantly, newspaper headlines going back ten years leap out at me, one after the other. Criminal investigations. Accusations of murder. Accusations of being part of the Russian mob.

I lead a large private security team. And made enough money at it to grow a small real estate empire.

The screen blurs, and I feel myself go cold as my sense of safety evaporates. *He's a mob enforcer.*

8

SERGEI

"It's the mother. I'm certain of it." I'll have to tell Catherine as soon as she wakes up. I pace across my bedroom excitedly, talking into my phone. "Morty's mother was one of the people who tried to sue, was she not?"

"Yes," Xenia replies in her cool voice. "She has also been in and out of mental hospitals for the last fifteen years." I hear keys clicking. "Delusional disorder. She believes that Morty's spirit possesses her part time."

"All right, listen." My heart is pounding. The more time I spend with Catherine, the more devoted I find myself to her protection. I still don't know how I will acquaint her to the reality of who I am and what I do, but I must try.

And if there is one thing that should make her take the news more favorably, it will be stopping her stalker once and for all.

"Mikhail has already placed another six men under my supervision to go with my dozen. All are to be given photographs and information about the mother and her delusions. She is the new target. She may be dressed like Morty, as she is in the third photograph."

The woman has gone all out in her effort to look like her

"possessing" son. Her hair has been clipped short like his and dyed that same dark-walnut brown. She wears a man's overlarge fedora and trench coat that I quickly match to the ones in Marty's picture, and in every picture, her face is blank of any expression.

"I will distribute the materials," Xenia promises. "Good catch, Sergei."

"And yourself." I hang up the call, smiling—just as Boris bursts in out of breath with a look of anger and panic on his broad face.

"Sergei—it's your girl! She snuck out of her room. We caught her slipping out the door on the security cameras, but the storm's obscuring visibility outside and we lost her." He starts in on an apology, but I am already racing out past him, heading for the stairs down to the first floor. I should be angry—furious that she has broken her promise to stay with me and outraged that she would be so cavalier about her own safety. Instead, I am afraid. Both that Morty will find her before I do and that she knows all and will never forgive me my secrets.

Catherine. I'm so sorry. There is so much I have not told her. My life. My family.

The harrowing journey to the States so that my mother could get proper care after my father's death. My debt to Mikhail for getting us here, and how I ended up paying it off by bloodying my hands.

How all I want is something clean in my life—a wife, a family, and something to come home to which is untainted by my bloody work. How the adoration in her eyes leaves me hopeful, for the first time in my life, that it might be possible.

I race into the storm coatless, pistol hidden against my side, determined to find Catherine before Morty's deranged mother does.

The rain soaks me through in seconds as I look up and down

the street. I don't know what drove Catherine to flee her room, but I know that her stalker will either be watching the building or having it watched.

I get back on the phone as I stalk toward the nearest subway station, knowing she'll have trouble getting a taxi in this mess. I'm already barking orders, calling my men in to form a dragnet around the area. We have to get to her before her would-be assassin catches her and smuggles her out of the area.

I can't fail Catherine. *I can't lose her.*

It's pure chance that makes the wind drop enough that I hear muffled cries of protest under it. I look around again, straining my ears, and hear the small sound again, echoing out from a nearby alley. I turn down it, stepping into the shadows and letting my eyes adjust.

There's a rental van parked down the alley with the back doors hanging open. Two figures struggle in front of it, one slim and smaller, one big, blocky, and draped in a long coat. I move forward quickly and quietly, feeling a volcanic surge of rage rising up inside of me.

9

CATHERINE

It all happened so fast. I tried to sneak out without anyone noticing, but someone had been watching the entrance, even in the storm that had blacked out half the block. As I stepped out into the blowing rain, distracted by a breaking heart and sheer panic, someone had come up behind me and tucked a knife under my chin.

I STARTED TO ZONE OUT, caught in a flashback, and went limp as she dragged me down the block and around into a narrow, shadowed alley. My head filled up with the explosion: my father dissolving like a burnt-paper outline a moment before my mother knocked me down and shielded me with her burning body.

BUT THEN SHE took the knife away from my neck and the strangest thing happened. I remembered Sergei's demand that I not treat his possessions—that I not treat *myself*—like trash. And even though I had run from him, I listen.

I run for it as she pulls the van doors open, and she drops the knife and runs to grab me and drag me back. I fight her, crying out before she can cover my mouth. And just as she raises a fist to start beating me into submission, we both hear a footstep behind us.

"Let her go." Sergei's voice is a growl that rises above the sound of the storm and makes my captor's blank face twitch with sudden nervousness. He is the eye of the storm—the calm center of the hurricane—and I suddenly feel safe in spite of the danger I'm still in.

"She's mine," the woman snaps, trying to grab me by the throat. I bite her hand and slam both handcuffed fists into the side of her face, and she staggers back. But before I can bolt toward Sergei's shadowy form, she grabs me by the hair and yanks me back against her.

"I said she's mine! My boy is dead! He won't let me rest until somebody pays!" The woman's throaty screech hurts my ear, and I'm too terrified to stop and wonder what she's talking about.

Sergei raises his pistol, his eyes narrowed. "Your boy died fifteen years ago, along with this poor girl's parents, in an explosion caused by industrial sabotage. Her parents didn't kill your boy, damn you," he growled. "Nor did she. He was killed by the same disgruntled employee who was responsible for hundreds of other deaths."

. . .

FOR A MOMENT, the woman goes quiet, and I think that maybe Sergei has reached her. But, then, her grip on me tightens. "You're lying! My boy wants her! If I sacrifice her, he'll let me rest!"

SHE DRAWS another knife from her coat pocket, and I squirm frantically to get away from her. But before she can get the blade clear of her pocket, Sergei calls to me:

"DO YOU TRUST ME, LITTLE ONE?"

OUR EYES MEET across the distance, and I see the determination in his ...and how it mixes with a quiet plea. In spite of everything I now know, I see who the real Sergei is. I trust him. I ...love him, I admit to myself. And I nod.

"THEN BE STILL and close your eyes."

I DO, and as the woman brings the knife up toward my throat, Sergei fires twice.

SHE GOES RIGID, the knife slipping from her fingers. I don't even hear her let out her breath; she simply slides away from me and falls to the wet asphalt as I bolt toward Sergei. I don't look back.

HE PUTS AWAY his weapon and grabs me in a bear hug, our

soaked bodies pressed together hard enough that I can feel his heart pounding against my breasts. His mouth crashes down on mine, and we kiss fiercely as I dig the fingers of my handcuffed hands against his muscled belly.

"Don't hate me for killing her," he whispers harshly in my ear. "She couldn't live, Catherine. Tell me you understand why."

I look up into his amazing eyes and kiss him softly, hearing the plea in his words. "I don't hate you, Sergei. What you did, you did for me."

Something in him seems to relax, then, and he scoops me and carries me inside.

"Why did you go?" he asks me upstairs in the penthouse ten minutes later. I'm swimming around in a black, terrycloth bathrobe of his, which brushes softly against my bare, chilled skin, taking the damp away. My wet clothes are gone, taken away by one of his men.

I sit on the couch in my huge bedroom with him and struggle to find the words. "I realized who you are and I couldn't handle it. I'm sorry. I really should have stayed and talked to you, no matter what side of the law you are on."

"Does it bother you so much that I am a man of principle, but not a man of the law?" His gaze is gentle but steady.

"Only some. If I had relied on the police to protect me, I would be dead now. But you keep coming through for me. And I want to stay with you."

It scares me a little to admit this; being part of his world makes me nervous. But after just a few days, I have learned how good he is for me.

He cups my face, then slides his hand back through my hair, gripping it at my nape again and kissing me lingeringly. My freed hands slide up his chest through the gap in his matching bathrobe and I hear him take in a shivery breath.

I can't take it anymore. My cowardice and trust issues aren't my friends; they nearly got me killed tonight. As the kiss breaks, I force out my words in a low whisper against his lips. "Make love to me."

A feral growl escapes his throat and he lunges for me, catching me in his arms and pushing me firmly against the cushions. I go willingly, lying back under him while he buries his face in my neck. My cry is half relief as the starved, desperate feeling inside of me starts to fade.

He marks me with teeth and tongue, sucking warmth to the

surface of my skin and leaving me trembling and moaning under him. The sound only turns him on more; he grips me harder, and my hands slide inside his loosened robe to caress the muscle of his back as he marks me with his mouth.

I CAN HEAR my breath shivering as he leaves tingling spots of soreness all over my neck, one hand sliding under my robe to grip my hip. He's struggling to take his time, but I can feel him shuddering and rake my nails lightly down his back, then over his hips, murmuring encouragement. His need for me only adds to my own desire. I've never been wanted by any man before and I am suddenly glad. From here on out, I will be his and his alone.

HIS HANDS EXPLORE my skin slowly, like he's blind and trying to memorize every curve and fold with his fingertips. Now and again, he finds a spot that sends tingles through me and makes me whimper; the crease of my hip, my spine, or the slope of my belly as it runs down from my navel. When a certain caress makes me gasp, he remembers and repeats it until I'm limp and trembling under him.

THEN, both of his hands settle over my breasts and he starts to stroke and knead them. I gasp and let out another moan; no one has ever touched me there. I almost freeze up, but it feels too good, and I soon relax under his touch.

HIS FIRM, rough-smooth hands have me trembling and arching from pleasure in moments as he starts stroking my nipples. All the while, he's watching my face, sweeping his eyes over my body, and seeming to struggle for self-control. His fingers swirl, pinch, and tug at my sensitive flesh until my head falls back and I start panting hysterically.

HE RUNS his mouth over my breasts, groaning and covering them with kisses. A moment later his lips close around my nipple and a hard jolt of pleasure runs all through me. I arch my back under him, pressing my breasts up against his face, and grip his thighs with both my legs.

HE'S GOT complete control of me now. Every pull of his mouth makes me arch up toward him, pushing a moan from my mouth and making the hunger inside me grow. He knows it and teases me that way a long time, switching breasts now and again while I sob and dig my nails into his skin.

I'm aching for him now, my cunt throbbing, feeling empty and hungry inside. But instead of throwing himself over me, he gets up off of me suddenly and stands, staring down at me with bright eyes. His chest heaves as I stare up at him in confusion.

HE SCOOPS ME UP SUDDENLY, leaving the robe behind and dropping his own off his shoulders so it hangs by its tie around his waist. He carries me to the broad, canopied bed and tosses me onto it; I bounce on the mattress, giggling a little, and roll back over to look at him.

HE STANDS OVER ME, hair wild and broad chest heaving, untying the robe and letting it drop. His whole body gleams like polished stone, smooth skin over hard muscle. His cock is huge, nestled in a neatly-trimmed dark fuzz and standing thick and gleaming from his thighs.

I CATCH MY BREATH, but I reach for him despite my shock and that touch of virgin's fear. He climbs onto the bed after me, his eyes gleaming with lust, and I feel the head of his cock slide up the inside of my thigh. But instead of pushing into me, he stays crouched over me, reaching down to run his palm down my belly and rest it on my pussy.

HE GIVES IT A GENTLE SQUEEZE, then drums his fingers over it lightly. One fingertip slides up and down my aching slit, and then is joined by a second. They move upward and start to stroke me experimentally, sending fresh jolts of pleasure through me.

I SHOULD BE DOING something to him as well, I convince myself, and try to focus enough on my limbs to make my hands move. But as I start to stroke his sides and run my hands over his back, he shivers, then murmurs, "Put your hands over your head."

IT SURPRISES ME, but I obey immediately, stretching them out across the bedspread. He looks me in the eyes and says, "Do not move them."

MY EYES widen and then roll closed as he lowers his head to my breasts again, tonguing each of my nipples erect before starting to kiss lower. Meanwhile, he keeps stroking my clit, one of his long fingers sliding into me. I clench around it, its presence inside me intensifying the pleasure of his caresses.

I GET LOST in sensation and don't notice him pulling my bottom to the edge of the bed or crouching with my knees propped apart by his shoulders. I'm already starting to tremble uncontrollably when the caressing fingers are replaced by a firm and agile tongue.

I SCREAM in a breath and clench my fists around wads of the bedspread, hips moving in time to the swirls of his tongue. I can hear myself wailing with pleasure as my muscles tighten all over my body. Something is building up in my body, the sensation collapsing my mind inward until all I can feel is that intensifying joy.

HE SLIDES another finger into me a moment before my muscles start clenching around them on their own. Ecstasy detonates through me again and again, satisfying a deep need I had not even known about before tonight. I thrash and sob until finally the spasms pass, leaving me limp and trembling.

HE KEEPS TONGUING ME INSISTENTLY, arousing me again and driving me fast toward another peak. I push myself against him eagerly, and he rewards me by speeding up and growing a little rougher. This time I croon instead of screaming, and the pleasure ripples through me in long, sensual waves.

. . .

He still keeps going, even as I go limp as wet cotton and can't even keep my eyes open any more. But this time is different. This time, he brings me right up to the edge ...and then his mouth and hands withdraw from me.

My eyes fly open, and I see his face full of lust and determination as he bends over and pushes his cock deep into my body. I gasp and thrash under him, nearly cumming just from the pressure and the sensual way he moves his shaft inside of me. He goes slowly at first, but pushes hard, grinding against me until I start to feel the tension start gradually building again.

He groans through his teeth and speeds up, digging his fingers into my hips as he pounds into me. I'm almost there again, forgetting his order and clinging to him, sobbing endearments, and crying *yes, yes, yes* as he shouts wordlessly in unison. Harder and faster, our bellies slap together and the bedsprings creak as he loses control of his strength.

He pushes me deep into the mattress and the pressure sets me off again; I moan long and throaty as an orgasm rolls through my body a third time. I hear his long, growling cries as if from far off and feel his cock spasm hard inside my body.

I must have fainted, for when my eyes open again, I'm curled against his side and there is a blanket over us. The storm is rattling away at the windows as we lie there catching our breaths. Finally, he checks in with me. "Are you all right?"

. . .

I STRETCH and smile up at him softly, and the concern in his face is replaced with relief and drowsy pleasure. "I'm good. Better than good." I can hardly believe that earlier tonight I was almost kidnapped by a madwoman.

APPARENTLY GOOD SEX *is just as good medicine as a couple of tranquilizers. At least when it comes from Sergei.*

I'm drifting off in his arms when he says speculatively, "You know...we have four days left before your agreement with me ends."

"I'M NOT LEAVING after four days." The determination in my tone stuns me as much as the words. "I'm yours, Sergei. And you're mine."

THE SMILE that breaks across his face is everything I've ever wanted to see. "Yes, Catherine. You are mine. My love. My heart. And I am yours." Gathering me so close I can hear his heart pounding, he reveals his deepest secret. "I love you."

I HOLD HIM TIGHTLY, this strongest of men, and give him the sum of both our desires. "And I love you, Sergei." My eyes twinkle, easing some of the simmering tension in the room as his expression goes slack with astonishment. "Make love to me again." I have no trouble saying it a second time, or a third and fourth and fifth throughout the long night. In fact, I never have trouble saying it again. Nor does Sergei ever deny us what we both need.

The End

SIGN UP TO RECEIVE FREE BOOKS

Sign Up to Receive Free E-Books and Audiobook Codes.

Would you like to read **The Unexpected Nanny, Dirty Little Virgin** and **other romance books** for **free?**

You can sign up to receive these free e-books and audiobooks by typing this link into your browser:

https://www.steamyromance.info/free-books-and-audiobooks-hot-and-steamy/

Or this one:

https://www.steamyromance.info/the-unexpected-nanny-free/

PREVIEW OF THE ORPHAN NEXT DOOR

A Single Daddy Next Door Romance

By Alisha Star

∽

Blurb

Emily is too young for me, but I can't shake how much I want her. I want to rescue her from her isolation. I certainly want to rescue her from that gold-digging little creep James.

I want to love her and be loved by her, and wake up to her face every morning. And of course, I'd love to make her mine. Even if our age difference didn't make me hesitate, James is doing his best to get and stay in the way, even after Emily throws him out of her life. He's stalking her; he's stalking us. And he's way too interested in my little girl for comfort. I'm determined to have Emily in my arms, safe from him and from the world's other predators. And when I finally get what I want, it's paradise. For a while, I don't think twice about that little brat and his complaining. But James isn't done. And as Emily and I work toward our first of what we hope is many Christmases to come, he's going to take his revenge. *I'm a patient man. But when he endangers my lover and my little girl, it is time for a reckoning.*

After living a life of extreme poverty, knowing nothing but neglect and loneliness, young Emily Dawn has won the New York State Lottery and become a multi-millionaire. Having moved into the most modest house she can find in Woodstock, New York, she quickly develops a crush on her next door neighbor: self-made billionaire and single dad Grant Norton. They become fast friends, especially when his cute daughter, Molly, takes a liking to Emily.

But Emily has a problem. She's been dating the charming James Parrish: a handsome and age-appropriate young man from the neighborhood who's doing his best to seduce her and make her fall in love. Grant senses that something is wrong with the smarmy young man, but doesn't know if it's just his jealousy getting the better of him—as much as he tries to fight it, he can't help his attraction to the kind-hearted Emily. Determined to break Parrish's spell on her, Grant steps in—and the attraction between them ends up catching fire.

As their affair intensifies, they must figure out how to tell Grant's daughter, especially when Parrish starts to harass all three of them. Bent on revenge, the thwarted con artist finally resorts to trying to kidnap Molly. The lovers must join forces against him to protect the young girl, and sort out what is going on between them.

EMILY

As I stare out the window of my new mansion as a handsome man kisses my neck, the only thought in my head is that I wish he would stop distracting me. The thought shocks me as soon as it crosses my mind—James Parrish is beautiful, blond, and dashing—but it's true. There's something about his hands on me, his lips pressing softly and wetly on my pulse, which leaves me feeling soiled—like he's leaving behind some sticky residue wherever he touches.

He's trying harder than usual to be seductive, but after everything that's happened it's all I can do not to flinch away.

I have to hide my discomfort. Last time I begged off from having sex with him he demanded to know what was wrong with me. All normal girls want to fuck him once he puts the moves on them, or so he claimed.

I had to tell him that it must be the trauma from being on the streets, and the fact that I'm not used to being touched. But afterward I felt so much worse about myself that I've since made sure to never let on that I don't want him again. It's ridiculous that I have to work so hard to spare his feelings when we've only been together for a little while—and when he's never spared mine.

So I continue to let him kiss me and play with my tits through my sweater while I distract myself. I stare out past the drops of rain clinging to the glass and down the long, grassy hillside to my neighbor's back yard. Grant Norton is out there in the rain letting his two Golden Retrievers, Pogo and Mike, run. I smile to see him, a warmth running through me that James can't evoke any more.

The trick works; James chuckles, thinking my smile is meant for him, and pulls me closer, nuzzling my cheek as I hold him limply in my arms. He thinks I'm a slow starter when it comes to romance—and I am, having no real experience with sex or affection. But if I stay cold and still and don't smile, he'll get insulted again and sulk, and kick up drama.

So I look at Grant to get my heart racing—and since I can't have him, I turn around and settle for James.

"Aw, come on, Red, what's so interesting out there?" he wheedles, tugging at one of my strawberry blonde curls.

I look back at him and smile. "Everything."

It's true. After a life filled with institutional halls and filthy alleyways, my house in Woodstock is paradise. Looking out the window at all that green, gold, and crimson would soothe my soul even if Grant wasn't out there.

I drink him in with my gaze as I lie across the bottle-green velvet couch that dominates my living room. His tall, broad-shouldered form stands under a black umbrella as he tosses neon orange squeaky balls up the slope so the dogs can race after them. His dark hair ripples in the breeze along with his black overcoat; his strong face is a tanned blur at this distance, but I can picture his strong features in my mind.

Grant is the best part of living in Woodstock—besides being able to afford it, that is. After spending a chilly spring on the streets of Brooklyn, an amazing stroke of luck six months ago changed everything in my life. Now, I have a big house in the woods, a hot neighbor, a fridge full of food and a life to look forward to...once I recover from what I went through before it took a turn for the better.

Grant—watching him in his yard, talking to him, having lunch with him and his adorable daughter Molly—makes me happy to get up in the morning. His existence in my life reminds me of all I now have to be grateful for—and all I still wish I could have. His pale green eyes, so startling against his tanned skin, are full of kindness, and his smile is contagious. A few minutes of conversation with him helps my mood no matter how bad things get.

"Hey, are you listening, baby?" James whines, and I look back up into his blank blue eyes and force a smile.

"I'm sorry, I didn't really sleep. What did you say?"

He rolls his eyes, the corner of his mouth turning up. James is almost ethereally beautiful, with smooth skin and the face of a marble angel. I used to find that babyish look cute, but I'm starting to get tired of it—along with his whiny tone when he wants something. "I said, baby, order us up some pizza! I'm getting the munchies, and I know you haven't eaten all day."

He's right about that last part. I'm still getting used to the idea that I can fill my belly whenever I want, and have a bad habit of neglecting that need. It's almost as disorienting as looking at my account statements and wondering at all those zeros. It all still seems so...foreign...to be able to satisfy my hunger whenever I need to.

"Okay, okay." I dig in my pocket to see what cash I have: none. I usually don't carry much cash around. It's an old habit too, but this one's too smart to leave behind. "I can make the order but I have no cash on me. Can you get the tip?"

It's a simple request—it's only five dollars. But the petulant look on his face deepens, making my heart sink immediately. "Oh, come on, baby, you know I'm broke until my app rolls out. It's just another few weeks. And I know you're good for it." He gives a charming smile, and my stomach clenches with the sudden urge to tell him to *go away for good*. I know I have more options in the romance department than James wants me to think.

But no matter how many options I may have, none of them are the one I want. None of them are Grant, who is a widower twice my age with a little daughter, and who, as far as I can tell, does not date. I've had a crush on him since I moved in here, well before James got in my face two months ago and refused to leave.

James tells me that he's crazy in love with me. He tells me that there's never been anyone like me before, and that he wants to spend the rest of his life with me. Then he comes over and plants himself on my couch for hours, pushing for sex, expecting to be fed, and always asking for money.

I don't know what love is supposed to feel like, exactly, but I'm pretty sure it's not meant to feel like this. I think it's supposed to be more like how I feel when I'm around Grant, or when I see him with his daughter. All warm inside—with no reservations.

Right now, there's a chill deepening in my womb as I sit up, using it as an excuse to pull away from him. "Fine," I sigh. "What kind of pizza do you want?"

"Hawaiian, you know what I like." He waves his beer at me like he's ordering from a servant, and I shake my head as I pull out my phone. Pineapple doesn't belong on pizza.

I order a medium chicken pesto with mushrooms and olives for myself and a medium Hawaiian for him. I have stocked the fridge with beer, though I barely touch the stuff myself. I'm kind of hoping he'll get whiskey dick tonight and leave me alone.

I know deep down that these are not the sort of things that a girl should be thinking about with her first official boyfriend. But even though I'm nineteen and he's in his twenties, James is definitely the less mature one in our relationship. He's very charming when he wants to be, but right now it's clear to me what he thinks. He thinks he's won me and that he doesn't have to put in any effort at all to keep me.

But is he wrong? *Why am I still putting up with this?*

I already know. I don't like thinking about it. Part of it is that horrible, empty ache of loneliness that will yawn inside of me like a canyon the moment he leaves. The other is a deeper worry, but one that has nagged at me more and more—*what if he won't leave when I tell him to?*

I place the pizza order and put the tip on my card along with everything else. By the time I look back outside again, Grant is gone.

"So, baby doll, how much time do we have to...play...before our food gets here?" James drapes his hand over my shoulder and reaches down to cup my breast through my pale pink sweater. He gives it a squeeze that he thinks is friendly, and while it doesn't hurt, I have to force myself not to squirm.

"Twenty minutes," I make up, knowing it's more like forty, and he grunts in disgust.

"That's too little time," he grumbles.

"Hey, you were the one who wanted pizza," I remind him, and he finally shrugs and nods.

"Okay, fine. I'll just fuck you twice later." He offers a sleazy grin, and it's all I can do to force an answering smile.

GRANT

"Is Emily coming over to trick or treat with us?" Molly wrinkles her nose as I dab on her grease paint. She decided to go as a cat burglar this year, which, to her nine-year-old mind means a fuzzy white and cream kitty outfit with a robber's mask across her eyes.

"I'm going to ask her, though I don't know if she's had time to come up with a costume. Hold still, sweetie, I'm trying to get your kitty nose straight." Her whiskers were hard enough. Molly is incredibly energetic; even channeling it into martial arts training hasn't cured her of the wiggles.

But squirminess won't stop me. I'm determined to do daddy-daughter costumes justice. And thus, I am going trick-or-treating with Molly as Macavity from *Old Possum's Book of Practical Cats,* one of her favorites.

. . .

IT TOOK some planning behind her back, but it turned out well, and Molly squealed when she saw it. A cosplayer friend made it for me. I'm dressed in a black Victorian evening suit, with a stripy orange tail hanging out between its coattails, a top hat with kitty ears, another robber mask, and white gloves. I drew the line at face paint.

WOODSTOCK IS TINY, its houses scattered; anyone who wants a real trick-or-treat haul in the eastern Catskills has to be willing to drive from town to town. That is more than fine with me—I love to drive, and I am hoping to take my sweet neighbor Emily with us.

EMILY IS BEAUTIFUL AND KIND, but she has no one. She's modest and hard-working as well, and Molly loves her. As for me...I'm starting to as well. If it wasn't for our huge age difference, I would love to pursue more than friendship with her.

But that's not why I want to take her along tonight. It's a lot more complicated than that, actually. I want her with me because I'm trying to pry loose a giant, smarmy blond leech that has attached himself to her.

EMILY IS YOUNG AND BIG-HEARTED, but clearly traumatized and new to having money and a place to stay. The new boyfriend, James somebody, has circled in on her like a shark smelling blood in the water. He's local and a little notorious—a slacker with half a job delivering bread on his bike three seasons and shoveling driveways one. Like a lot of the spoiled sons of rich Woodstock residents, he lives on other people's money, and only works so his mother doesn't know how much weed he's buying.

. . .

WOODSTOCK IS BIG ON GOSSIP, especially when there's dirt to sling around. James is the son of a Hollywood producer and his trophy wife—his rich dad stashes him here with his mom to keep them out of the spotlight. James, who lives with his mother (with whom he shares a forgettable last name) between girlfriends, looks to be trying to make himself into a trophy husband.

I HATE gold diggers of either sex. It's one of the reasons I have never remarried. Molly deserves to have two parents, but at least my wealth allows me to stay at home for her—except when one of my businesses has an important meeting, of course. And now, thanks to Emily, I don't even have to worry about vetting a stranger to babysit Molly while I'm gone.

I WISH I could shake my growing desire to keep her.

AS EASY AS it would be to place the blame on anyone else, I can't say it's entirely Molly's fault that I started becoming attracted to my nineteen-year-old neighbor. She didn't mean to put the idea in my head when she told me I should marry Emily so she could stay and take care of both of us. She just likes Emily and wants to keep her too.

Molly does not remember her mother, and I'm very glad of that. When we separated, Alicia said that going through with giving me a daughter was what had ruined our relationship. I don't fully understand her reasoning, but she complained that having a baby made her feel "too old."

The Virgin's Bargain

. . .

I URGED her to get counseling. I suspect to this day that it was postpartum depression. She simply wasn't like that before—wasn't like that when I fell in love with her. But Alicia was stubborn, and too proud. She refused to acknowledge that she had a problem.

I STILL REMEMBER the night she broke down and started shouting at me while Molly wailed in her bassinet, still too tiny to have any idea what was going on. She hated me, she hated Molly, she hated being sore and having stretch marks, and she hated her life with us most of all. I demanded that she seek treatment before her behavior started endangering herself and our baby, and she just laughed at me.

I ENDED up doing all the caring for Molly while Alicia refused to bond with her. Three months later she simply...drifted out of our lives. I woke up, she was gone, her things were gone, and our joint account had been cleaned out.

I WENT a little crazy trying to find her; her family wasn't cooperative, and the private investigators I hired turned up nothing. I had a newborn and felt, at the beginning, that Molly needed her mother. But Alicia vanished for an entire year before resurfacing again—in an obituary.

PERSISTENCE and a few bribes had gotten me the full police and coroner's reports. Molly's mother, whom I had loved for half my adult life, had been found semi-nude on a beach in Majorca. She had died out on the beach that lovely night, of what may have been a deliberate overdose on uncut cocaine and medical-grade morphine.

FURTHER INVESTIGATION INDICATED that she had spent the year and our money jet-setting around Europe pursuing every pleasure she could get her hands on—unaccompanied by anyone regularly, and contacting no one from her old life. She had been hospitalized for two previous suicide attempts: one in London and one in Amsterdam.

I'VE ALWAYS SHIELDED Molly from the truth about her mother. She only knows that her mother is dead. Not that she abandoned us and destroyed herself. And certainly not that I half blame myself for not taking steps to get Alicia into inpatient treatment before she disappeared.

SINCE THEN I'VE left off dating, focusing on two things: raising my daughter, and getting my head back together after learning the truth about Alicia. I don't rattle easy, but that genuinely haunts me. I didn't want to go into a new relationship dragging a lot of baggage, so I haven't even thought about it until recently.

THEN ALONG CAME EMILY. And now I think about it all the time. Seeing Emily bond with Molly in a way that Alicia never could makes it even harder not to imagine her as a permanent part of my life—of our lives.

. . .

But Woodstock loves gossip, and I know what would happen if I actually made Emily that kind of offer. The idea of a rich billionaire marrying a girl half his age, who also happens to be his babysitter, would be tasty gossip-fodder. I don't care what the local biddies think of me, but Emily and Molly would have to live with any fallout as well. To spare them, I've forced myself to avoid even the semblance of flirting.

But I do care for Emily, and I do really want her. She's a good person, and she deserves to have people around her who care about her. Instead, she's sticking with that leech James, who is taking advantage of her inexperience and loneliness.

It's the one thing about her that frustrates me, and I can't blame her for it. Her heart is too big, and she expects too little from others. Far less than I would give her if I had the chance.

I rarely want to punch a guy in the face on first meeting, but this James guy gets to me. I've had a close encounter with someone like him before. Just thinking of James pawing at Emily in public makes my back teeth ache.

Emily may not be mine, but someone has to look after her. That may mean stepping in where James is concerned, so I'm always watchful. I don't want to get in her business unless invited, but I'll chuck all decorum out the window if he hurts her.

I step back and look at Molly, whose cream stripes and little pink nose are all even now. "There we go. Go have a look." I point at the full-length mirror across the bright bathroom, and she hurries over to it and squeals.

I LOSE the fight against grinning. "So did I do good?"

"DEFINITELY AN A+ JOB, Daddy. Now are we gonna pick up Emily?" She rocks on her heels, and my smile fades. I'm a little worried that Emily's too caught up in James's web and will let him keep her home.

"LET me call her and find out when." I don't want to presume and end up putting both Emily and Molly at the center of a tense and awkward scene. I punch in Emily's number as we walk out of the bathroom toward the rambling Victorian mansion's giant living room.

BOTH OUR GOLDENS sprawl out on the couch. I spent two good hours wearing them out by throwing balls and letting them run up and down the grassy slope that separates Emily's house from my own. Neither of them raises their head as we come in, but both start thumping their tails against the couch cushions. Molly goes over to pet them while I wait for Emily to pick up.

IT TAKES THREE RINGS. As I wait, I feel my blood pressure going up as I imagine her with James, trying to answer the phone. James pulling the phone out of her hands and going back to whatever inept sex act he's imposing on her.

I HAVE SEEN her discomfort at the way he paws at her in public. If there was ever a rosy glow of new love between them, he must have spoiled it quickly with all his ass-grabbing antics. My sister Catherine is still on permanent vacation in Majorca, recovering from the scars that her own version of James left her with. As for my brother—he's always been a version of James.

WHEN EMILY PICKS UP FINALLY, all the air whooshes out of me in relief. "Whoo. Hey. Uh, it's Grant. Molly wants to know if you'll come trick-or-treating with us."

"OH...OH HI!" Her voice perks up at once, and suddenly I'm calm again, feeling a mix of warm fuzzies in my chest area and a tightening in my groin. "Um, well, I—" she starts, and I hear the sudden, worried hesitation in her voice. "I'd like to."

I HEAR RUSTLING in the background—and then a door opens. "Who is it, babe?" says a young man's voice, and my eyes narrow in annoyance.

"MY NEIGHBOR NEEDS a hand taking his little girl trick or treating," she replies in a voice that sounds a touch too cheery. My smile goes lopsided at her small display of cunning. I never said anything about *needing* her help with Molly, but if anybody asks me I'll back her story in a second.

. . .

"What? Aw, come *on*, baby, you have a boyfriend now. You've gotta stay home and take care of me!" His deep voice wheedles like a kid's.

"Take care of you? You're a grown—" she sighs and I hear her stop to take a deep breath before going on. *Just go ahead and yell at him, honey, he deserves every bit of it.*

But she doesn't, instead answering him with frustrating patience. "Look, James. We already talked about this. You're going to your mom's tonight." She speaks slowly and carefully, as if to a child with a volatile temper, and my heart sinks.

"Fuck my mom. I want the—" he starts, laughing off her concerns, trying to sound charming. He's the kind of guy who is used to letting his pretty face get him what he wants, just like his mother. "She'll be drunk by three in the afternoon anyway, she'll pass out before the servants bring out dinner. It doesn't matter."

"James, I sat there and listened to you promise her," she urges, but he just laughs some more. I hear rustling again and a small sound of discomfort from her, and a hot flush of rage runs through me.

Let her go, you son of a bitch. I want to say it aloud, but yelling through a phone is pointless. Should I go up the hill and rescue her from Mr. Won't-Take-No-For-An-Answer's grubby paws? I hesitate, my fist clenched, wanting to do just that.

. . .

THEN, a small hand tugs at my pant leg. I look down and see Molly gazing up at me solemnly. She holds her hand out for the phone. I shake my head, but she stamps her foot insistently. "I've got a plan, Dad."

I PAUSE, wondering what my imp is up to, and then hand her the phone.

MOLLY LISTENS FOR A MOMENT, frowns tremendously, sticks her finger in her ear and yells "*I wanna talk to Emily right now!*"

THE ARGUMENT over the phone stops at once, and I'm suddenly grinning again. I should be telling her that that's not an inside voice. I don't.

SHE SMILES. "Hi Emily! We're dressed as kitties and we need you to come help us trick-or-treat. So tell your stupid boyfriend to go back to his mommy! You've got other friends and he's just being selfish!"

MY GRIN FADES and I stare. My daughter surprises me regularly these days, but this one's a big one. *How are you nine?*

ON THE OTHER end of the phone, Emily is laughing, and I hear James go "aw shit" almost sheepishly. Cute plus angry can be a potent combination. "Duty calls, sweetie. We've already got plans for tomorrow anyway, and you're out of clothes."

. . .

"Now that wouldn't happen if you let me leave some stuff here," he complains, but she cuts him off gently.

"James, I haven't even gotten used to living indoors yet, give me time before I give up my privacy entirely, okay?" Her voice is tender and patient...and is the exact same voice she uses with my nine-year-old.

Unfortunately, James is less reasonable than even Molly at her angriest and most overtired. "Oh come on, don't be a coward. I love you! We should be together. All the time."

You mean, "Your money and I should be together all the time," you damned parasite. My back teeth are still grinding together, and I hold myself still as Molly hands me the phone. *Don't do it Emily* I mouth, but if he hears me he'll make even more trouble for her.

"You shouldn't call me names," she says quietly. It's something Molly says to mean kids on the playground, but in Emily's mouth it is grave and edged with tension. James starts to stammer an answer, but she simply raises the phone back to her ear. "I need to get changed. You're doing cats?"

"Uh...yes, cat burglars, actually."

. . .

SHE LAUGHS A LITTLE. "That's cute. Pick me up in fifteen minutes?"

I GIVE MOLLY A THUMBS-UP, and snort as she bounces in place. "Sounds good. See you then."

SHE HANGS UP, cutting off James in the middle of a protest, and I tuck my phone away, chuckling. *James zero, Emily and people who actually care about her, one.*

"SO WHEN DO we pick her up?" Molly asks, eyes bright with anticipation.

"WE LEAVE IN TEN MINUTES," I announce cheerfully.

"YAY!" She hugs me around my waist, and we sit down on the couch to pet the dogs as we wait.

Twelve minutes later, we pull up to the curb outside Emily's house. It's one of the other huge old Victorians dotting the woods around Woodstock. She's having the old house refurbished bit by bit while she lives in it. They're not going to finish by winter, but all rooms are livable, and some are already gorgeously restored.

SHE TOLD me once that the house was like her; falling apart in some places, but becoming new and lively again. No wonder

James keeps trying to move in there, while she struggles to keep him out.

When I first found out that a New York State Lottery winner was moving in next door, I expected some brash, newly rich kid. Someone a little bit like James. Instead I got Emily—endlessly grateful for every bit of her new life.

She's told me only a little of the nightmares she's gone through, but I can see a lot of it in her eyes still. She has the haunted expression of someone who's spent most of her life so isolated and starved for love that even crappy, fake, fast-food romance like the kind James is offering feels good to her.

The door bangs open seconds after I pull up, and I see James come stomping out. He doesn't seem to notice my white SUV, which has darkened windows. Hands shoved deep in his pockets, he turns the corner and walks quickly down the street, shoulders hunched against the deepening cold.

I watch him, fighting the urge to laugh at him as he retreats back to his mother's house where he belongs. He disappears around the corner at the end of the street, and I sigh with relief. *Well, that's one problem out of the way. Temporarily, anyway.*

Then the door opens again, and I look up, my heart lifting. Emily comes out, her strawberry blonde curls shining in the dying sunlight, a pink puffy overcoat not quite concealing her slim curves. She's not in costume, but as her soft sea-blue eyes settle on my SUV and light up, I see she has a sparkly-tipped cat teaser toy in her hand.

If you want to continue reading this story, you can get your copy from your favorite vendor by searching for the title:

<u>The Orphan Next Door</u>
<u>A Single Daddy Next Door Romance</u>

You can also find the e-book version by typing this link in your computer's browser:

<u>https://www.hotandsteamyromance.com/products/the-orphan-next-door-a-single-daddy-next-door-romance</u>

OTHER BOOKS BY THIS AUTHOR

Saving Her Rescuer: A Billionaire & A Virgin Romance

I was just trying to get away from my crazy ex for the weekend when I ended up in a giant pileup on the highway up to Gore Mountain.

https://geni.us/SavingHerRescuer

∽

Sensual Sounds: A Rockstar Ménage

Lust. Lies. Double lives.

The rock and roll industry is full of people who are looking out for themselves and willing to do anything to rise to the top.

https://www.hotandsteamyromance.com/collections/frontpage/products/sensual-sounds-a-rockstar-menage

∽

On the Run: A Secret Baby Romance

Murder. Lies. Fraud. Just another day in the lives of billionaires and women on the run.

https://www.hotandsteamyromance.com/collections/frontpage/products/on-the-run-a-secret-baby-romance

∽

The Dirty Doctor's Touch: A Billionaire Doctor Romance

I am a master. An elitist. I am at the top of my field, and I know what I am doing.

https://www.hotandsteamyromance.com/collections/frontpage/products/the-dirty-doctor-s-touch-a-billionaire-doctor-romance

∼

The Hero She Needs: A Single Daddy Next Door Romance

He's the only man I've ever wanted...

https://www.hotandsteamyromance.com/collections/frontpage/products/the-hero-she-needs-a-single-daddy-next-door-romance

∼

You can find all of my books here:

Hot and Steamy Romance

https://www.hotandsteamyromance.com

∼

Facebook

facebook.com/HotAndSteamyRomance

COPYRIGHT

©Copyright 2020 by Eliza Duke - All rights Reserved
In no way is it legal to reproduce, duplicate, or transmit any part of this document in either electronic means or in printed format. Recording of this publication is strictly prohibited and any storage of this document is not allowed unless with written permission from the publisher. All rights are reserved.
Respective authors own all copyrights not held by the publisher.

www.ingramcontent.com/pod-product-compliance
Lightning Source LLC
LaVergne TN
LVHW011731060526
838200LV00051B/3132